RAINBOW MAGIC:
GOLDIE THE SUNSH

There's trouble afoot in Fairyland –
Jack Frost has stolen the Weather
Fairies' magic feathers!

...idie the Sunshine Fairy is all hot
and bothered without her shimmery
sunshine feather. Can Rachel and
Kirsty seek it out and put a stop to
a sticky situation?

First published in Great Britain in 2004
by Orchard Books
This Large Print edition published 2008
by BBC Audiobooks Ltd
by arrangement with
Orchard Books

ISBN: 978 1405 662857

HiT entertainment

British Library Cataloguing in Publication Data available

Goldie
the Sunshine Fairy

Daisy Meadows

Illustrated by Georgie Ripper

The Fairyland Palace

Forest of

Sweet Factory

The Village Hall

River

Wetherbury Village

Far

Jack Frost's Ice Castle

reen Wood

Mrs. Fordham's Cottage

The Park

Willow Hill

The High St.

The Museum

rsty's ouse

rd

Mudhole

Fields

N
←W   E→
S

Goblins green and goblins small,
I cast this spell to make you tall.
As high as the palace you shall grow.
My icy magic makes it so.

Then steal Doodle's magic feathers,
Used by the fairies to make all weathers.
Climate chaos I have planned
On Earth, and here, in Fairyland!

Dedicated to Liss Brothwell,
who is a little ray of sunshine

Special thanks to
Sue Mongredien

Contents

A Sunny Spell

'I feel as if I'm about to melt,'
said Rachel Walker happily.

It was a hot summer afternoon and
she and her friend, Kirsty Tate, were
enjoying the sunshine in Kirsty's
back garden. A bumblebee buzzed
lazily around Mrs Tate's sunflowers,
and a single breath of wind
whispered through the yellow
rose bushes.

1

The weather had been so warm and sunny, Mr and Mrs Tate had given the girls permission to camp out in the garden that night. Kirsty looked up from a jumble of tent poles and bright orange material she was sorting through. 'It's been a perfect day,' she agreed. 'Let's hope tonight is perfect, too. I don't fancy lying out here in the rain, do you?' Rachel laughed, and started untangling tent pegs with her friend. 'I think I'd rather have a shower in the morning, not in the middle of the night,' she agreed.

Kirsty held up some poles. 'Right.

How do we put this thing together, then?' she asked brightly.

Rachel scratched her head. 'Well...' she began.

'Need some help?' came a voice from behind them.

'Dad!' said Kirsty in relief. 'Yes, please. We—' She burst out laughing as she looked at her father.

Rachel turned to see what was so funny. She had to bite her lip not to laugh, too. For there, standing in front of them, was Mr Tate, wearing the most enormous sunglasses she had ever seen.

Mr Tate was looking very pleased. He waggled the glasses up and down on his nose. 'Do you like my new shades?' he asked.

'Well, yes,' Kirsty said, trying to keep a straight face. 'They're very... summery.'

Mr Tate knelt down and started putting the tent together. 'The weather has been strange all week, I didn't know whether to buy them or not,' he said. 'I hope it doesn't start snowing again!'

Rachel and Kirsty looked at each

other but didn't say anything. They shared a very special secret. They knew why the weather had been so strange – Jack Frost had been messing it all up.

Doodle, the fairy weather-vane cockerel, usually looked after the weather with his seven magic tail feathers. But Jack Frost had cast a spell to make his goblin servants bigger and sent them to steal Doodle's feathers. Without them, the weather had gone completely haywire. Rachel and Kirsty were helping the Weather Fairies to get them back, but until that time, Doodle was just an ordinary iron weather-vane on top of the Tates' barn.

Yesterday, with the help of Pearl the Cloud Fairy, Kirsty and Rachel had returned the Cloud Feather to Doodle. But there were still four feathers left to find.

'There!' said Mr Tate, stepping back and admiring the finished tent. 'It's all yours.'

'Thanks, Dad,' Kirsty said as he walked away. She put two sleeping bags inside the tent and then flopped down on the grass. 'Phew!' she whistled. 'It's still so hot! I hope it cools down soon, or we'll never be able to sleep in there.'

Rachel was frowning and looking at her watch.

'Kirsty,' she said slowly. 'Have you noticed where the sun is?'

Kirsty looked up and pointed. 'Right there, in the sky,' she replied helpfully.

'Yes, but look how high it is,' Rachel insisted. 'It hasn't even setting yet.'

Kirsty glanced at her watch. 'But it's half-past seven,' she said. Now she was frowning, too. 'So that can't be right.'

Rachel had just opened her mouth to reply, when suddenly there was a loud Pop! 'What was that?' she whispered.

Pop! Pop! Pop!

'It sounds like it's coming from the

other side of the hedge,' Kirsty answered, her eyes wide. 'But there's only a cornfield over there.'

Pop! Pop! Pop!

Curiously, the girls peeped over the hedge to see what was making all the noise. And then they both gasped out loud.

Goldie Drops In

'I don't believe it,' Kirsty said,
rubbing her eyes. 'Is that
what I think it is?'

Pop! Pop! Pop!

Rachel nodded. 'Popcorn,'
she breathed.

It was an amazing sight. The sun
was so hot that the corn in the field
was literally cooking – and turning

into popcorn! Both girls stared
as golden puffs of corn
bounced everywhere.
It was just as if
the field was one
enormous saucepan.
A delicious smell
of popcorn
drifted over the
hedge, and
both girls
sniffed hungrily.

Kirsty and Rachel
looked at each other,
and grinned.

'There's definitely
magic in the air,'
Kirsty said.

'It must be the goblin
with the Sunshine Feather,'
Rachel agreed, feeling her
heart beat faster with excitement.

Both girls peered hard at the field, hoping to spot a goblin lurking somewhere, but it was difficult to see clearly through the blizzard of popcorn. It was still tumbling and twirling in the sky, like a sandstorm. Rachel suddenly grabbed Kirsty's hand. 'Look!' she cried. Kirsty stared. Darting above the corn was a twinkling yellow light. It was

11

zigzagging through the air between
the flying pieces of popcorn and
heading straight towards them.
As it came closer, the air above
the field seemed to glitter with
a thousand tiny sparkles. Both
girls could see a pair of delicate
golden wings beating quickly,
and the glimmer of a tiny wand.

'It's Goldie the Sunshine Fairy,' whispered Rachel in delight.

They held their breath as the fairy weaved in and out of the bouncing corn, neatly dodging each piece. Then she swooped down to land on the hedge in front of them. 'Phew!' she laughed. 'Talk about a bumpy ride!'

Kirsty and Rachel watched as Goldie shook popcorn dust from her glittering, golden-edged wings. Her face was framed by long, curly, blonde hair, and she wore a gauzy dress in fiery reds, yellows and oranges. A tiny gold tiara glinted in her hair and shiny red bangles glimmered on her wrists.

'Hello again,' said Goldie. 'I've been hearing all about how you've helped Crystal, Abigail and Pearl. You've done brilliantly!'

Rachel and Kirsty grinned at each other proudly. 'The goblin who has the Sunshine Feather can't be far away,' Goldie went on, looking up at the sky where the sun was still blazing as brightly as ever.

'That's what we thought,' Kirsty said. 'There's a farm on the

other side of this field. Shall
we start looking there?'

'Good idea,' Goldie replied
cheerfully. But then her face fell
as she looked at the cornfield
again. Popcorn was still whizzing
around like hot white missiles.
'Is there another way across
the field, though?'

Goblin on the Loose!

Goldie sighed. 'I don't fancy dodging that popcorn again,' she said. She leaned back to examine a scorch mark on one of her wings. 'I almost burned myself last time.'

'There's a lane that runs down the side of the field to the farm,' Kirsty told her. 'We'll ask Mum if we can go for a quick walk before bedtime.'

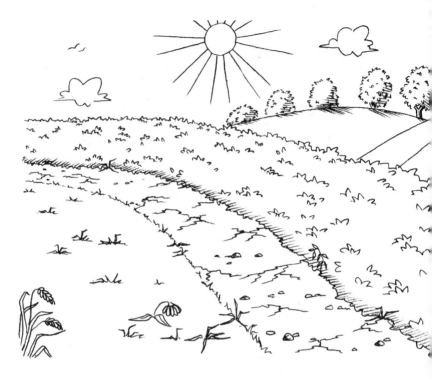

Minutes later, the three of them were on their way. The air was practically shimmering with heat. There were cracks in the ground where the earth had become hardened by the sun, flowers wilted in the hedgerow, and the grass was turning dry and brown. There wasn't even the slightest gasp of wind now.

Once they reached the farm,
the girls and Goldie started
searching for the goblin.

First they peeped into the stables.
Two very hot-looking horses were
sheltering from the sun. 'Hello,'
Goldie said. 'I don't suppose
you've seen a goblin hanging
around, have you?'

One of the horses shook her mane.

'All we've seen is this stable,'
she said. 'And there are
no goblins in here.'

'It's too hot to go out,' the
other horse whinnied.

Next, the girls and Goldie slipped into the cowshed. The cows were all half-asleep in the heat, and quite grumpy at being disturbed. There was no goblin.

At last the three friends came to the duck pond. They wondered if the goblin might be cooling off in the water, but there was no sign of him – or the Sunshine Feather.

'You should ask the pigs,' a duck quacked helpfully from a shady spot in the reeds.

'They've been

grumbling all day about something or other. And pigs are nosy. If there's a goblin on the farm, they'll know about it.'

Goldie thanked the duck politely.

'I think I can hear the pigs over here,' Rachel said, leading the way around the side of the farmhouse.

Soon they could all hear the grunting. The duck was right, the pigs seemed very upset about something. They all turned to look curiously at Goldie, though, when she flew over to speak to them. Goldie fluttered down to perch on the biggest pig's snout. 'What's the problem?' she asked kindly.

The pig squinted at the golden fairy in front of his little blue eyes. 'It's like this,' he began, in a cross, squeaky kind of voice. 'It's been so hot that the farmer topped up the mudhole with water, so that us pigs could keep nice and cool.' He twitched his ears indignantly. 'But someone else has pinched our spot in the mud – and he won't let us in!'

'It's not fair,' a piglet squealed, running up to Rachel and Kirsty. 'It's not fa-a-a-air!'

'It certainly isn't,' Kirsty agreed, giving him a pat.

'It sounds like just the kind of trick

a goblin would play!' Rachel pointed
out. 'Where is the mudhole?'

The pigs gave directions and the
girls set off with Goldie flying above
their heads. Rachel crossed her
fingers. She felt quite sure that
they would find a goblin in the
mud. Who else would be mean
enough to stop the pigs from
wallowing in their own mud pool?

They hadn't been walking for very
long when they heard someone

singing in a croaky, tuneless voice:

'I've been having so much fun
Blasting out this golden sun.
It's roasting, toasting,
popcorn weather.
Oh, how I love my
Sunshine Feather!'

Kirsty, Rachel and Goldie dived
behind a nearby tree at once, and
carefully peeped out. There, right

in the middle of the mudhole,
covered in thick, wet mud, was an
extremely cheerful goblin. He waved
the Sunshine Feather in the air as
he sang, and each time it moved,
golden sunbeams flooded from its
tip, making the air feel even hotter.

When he got to the end of his song, he started all over again, splashing his feet in the mud in time to the words. *'I've been having so much fun...'*

'What shall we do?' Kirsty whispered. The goblin was holding the feather so tightly, it looked like it would be impossible to take it from him.

Goldie twirled around in frustration.

'I hate seeing him with my Sunshine Feather,' she muttered, folding her arms across her chest. 'Look, he's got it all muddy!'

Rachel frowned. 'Maybe we could distract him somehow, then dash over and

grab the feather while
he's looking the other way.'

'I don't fancy dashing through all
that slippery mud,'
Kirsty said
quietly, eyeing
it doubtfully.
'We'll probably
fall over. And
look, he's right
in the middle of
it. He'll be able to
spot us coming way
before we get there.'

They drew further away
from the mudhole so that they could
discuss their next move without fear
of the goblin overhearing. After
a few minutes, Rachel held up
a hand. 'Ssshh! What's that
noise?' she hissed in alarm.

A Bamboozled Goblin

Kirsty, Rachel and Goldie held their breath as they listened to the strange new sound. It was a loud, wheezing, rumbling kind of noise, somewhere between a grunt and a hiss. Grumble-sshhh, it went. Grumble-sshhh. Grumble-sshhh...

It was coming from the direction of the mudhole. Kirsty and Rachel crept back to the tree and peeped out from behind it, wondering

what sort of terrifying creature
they were going to see.

When Rachel saw what was
making the noise, though, she had
to clap her hand over her mouth to
stop herself laughing out loud. The
wheezy rumble was nothing more
than the goblin – snoring!

'At least he isn't singing any
more,' Kirsty laughed.

Goldie fluttered her wings
hopefully when she saw that the
goblin was asleep, and she flew

a little closer to the Sunshine
Feather. But her face fell
when she saw just how
tightly the goblin was
clutching the feather
to his chest in his
sleep. She flew back
to the girls, shaking
her head. 'If I try and
pull it out of his grasp,
he's sure to wake up,'
she told them. 'How are we
going to get that feather?'

A smile appeared on Kirsty's face.
'Maybe we could...' she began
thoughtfully. Then she grinned
broadly. 'Yes! That could
work!' she declared.

Without another word, she began
running back towards her house.
'Back in a minute,' she called
over her shoulder.

Rachel and Goldie watched her go.
They were both dying to know what
Kirsty was up to. Luckily, they didn't
have to wait long for her return.
And when she came back, she
looked quite different!

'What *is* she wearing?' Goldie
murmured to Rachel as they saw
Kirsty running towards them.

'Her dad's sunglasses,' Rachel
replied, staring at her friend with

great interest. She was starting to wonder if Kirsty had been in the sun for too long. Why had she brought the enormous sunglasses with her? And why was she carrying a fishing rod?

Kirsty grinned at the confused expressions on their faces. 'I'll explain everything,' she promised, reaching up to rest the fishing rod in the tree. 'First, we need to shrink to fairy size, Rachel.'

Both Kirsty and Rachel had been given beautiful gold lockets by the Fairy Queen. Inside each locket was magical fairy dust. A tiny pinch of the sparkling dust was enough to turn the girls into fairies in the twinkling of an eye!

Kirsty and Rachel sprinkled themselves with fairy dust. It glittered a bright

sunshine-yellow in the light and then
– whoosh – they were getting
smaller and smaller and smaller.
The tree next to them became
enormous as the girls shrank
to the size of Goldie.

Kirsty and Rachel fluttered their
wings in delight. They both
loved being fairies.

'Now then,' Kirsty said. 'Fly up to the tree and I'll tell you my plan.'

They all perched by the fishing rod, and Goldie and Rachel watched as Kirsty's nimble fingers balanced the sunglasses on the end of the fishing hook.

'We're going to let the fishing line out slowly,' Kirsty told them quietly, 'and lower the sunglasses onto the goblin's nose.'

'Why?' Rachel wanted to know.

'Do you think they'll suit him?' Goldie asked.

Kirsty shook her head, trying not to laugh. 'With sunglasses on, everything will look dark to him,' she whispered. 'With a bit of luck, he'll think the Sunshine Feather has broken!'

Goldie clapped her hands in delight. 'Oh, what a good

idea!' she cried. 'I do love to play tricks on those mean old goblins.'

Very carefully, Kirsty, Rachel and Goldie turned the wheel of the fishing rod and lowered the sunglasses all the way down to the goblin. Kirsty held her breath as the sunglasses landed right on the end of his nose. Perfect!

They reeled in the fishing line and then Goldie waved her wand to release a stream of magical, sunny fairy dust. Little golden sparkles fizzed and popped like firecrackers around the goblin's head until he woke with a start.

He opened his eyes and blinked

when he saw that everything seemed
to have gone dark. 'My feather's
broken!' he moaned, giving it a shake.
'Shine, you stupid sun!'
he commanded.

Of course, the Sunshine Feather
wasn't broken at all. As soon as the
goblin shook it, the sun shone more
brilliantly than ever. But as far as
the goblin could see, the world
remained in darkness.

He waved the feather again.
'I said, shine!' he ordered, in

frustration. The sun shone obediently as if it were the middle of the day, but the goblin could see no change. Twice more he shook the feather and twice more the sun shone hotter and brighter, but through the sunglasses, the goblin saw only twilight. As far as he knew, the Sunshine Feather was having no effect. 'Broken!' the goblin finally announced crossly, and he threw the feather away in disgust.

Goldie shot out
of the tree at once,
like a little golden
firework. While
the goblin was
still muttering
gloomily to
himself, Goldie
swooped down
and grabbed the
feather. 'Thank
you!' she sang
happily, hugging
it tightly as she
flew back to the
girls. Kirsty's plan
had worked!

With another sprinkle
of fairy dust, Rachel and
Kirsty turned themselves human
again and started scrambling down
from the tree with the fishing rod.

The goblin spotted them and jumped to his feet. As he did so, the sunglasses bounced on his nose.

'Sunglasses?' he exclaimed, sounding puzzled as he reached up to grab the glasses. He pushed them onto the top of his head and peered at the girls, blinking in the dazzling sunlight. 'You tricked me!' he yelled in fury when he saw Goldie

clutching the Sunshine Feather.
'Come back with that feather!'

Kirsty and Rachel looked at
each other fearfully. Now that
Jack Frost's goblins were so big,
they seemed more scary than ever.
And this one looked very angry
at having been outwitted.

He shook his fist and ran
straight towards the girls.

'*Run!*' shouted Kirsty.

Happy Pigs

Rachel grabbed Kirsty's hand
and they both ran towards the
farmhouse as fast as they could.
The goblin was right behind them,
making a horrible growling
sound in his throat.

'Give me back that feather! Give
it back!' he screamed angrily.

Rachel's heart thumped painfully
in her chest as she ran. The goblin

45

was closing on them. She could hear his breathing, hoarse and ragged. The goblin stretched out his hand to grab her and she gasped as she felt his fingertips brush her shoulder.

'Got y—' he began. Then his voice turned from anger to confusion. 'Hey! What's happening?'

With a swirl of dancing sunbeams,

Goldie had waved the Sunshine Feather and pointed it straight at the goblin. At once, the sun beat down fiercely upon him – and the thick mud that smothered him started drying rapidly. As his legs became stiff and heavy with the solidifying mud, the goblin slowed. Then, as the mud set hard, the

goblin found he couldn't move at all.

'No-o-o-!' he wailed in despair.

Despite having been so scared just a few seconds earlier, the girls found themselves smiling at the sight of the goblin. 'He's a goblin statue!' Rachel exclaimed, laughing.

Only his eyes moved now. They flicked back and forth wildly as the goblin glared first at the girls, and then at Goldie who was fluttering beside them.

Kirsty noticed her dad's sunglasses on top of the goblin's head. She took a cautious step towards him. And another. The goblin remained motionless, so she marched right up to him and carefully took the glasses.

'I'll have these back now, I think,' she said. 'If I'd known how useful these sunglasses would be, I'd never have laughed at Dad for wearing them!' she told Rachel.

Goldie and the girls made their way back to the farmhouse where the pigs were waiting expectantly.

'The mudhole is all yours again,' Goldie said to the pigs in her sweet silvery voice. 'You'll find a new goblin scarecrow nearby,' she added. 'But don't worry. He won't be in any hurry to go back into the mud.'

The pigs grunted joyfully and started trotting off in search of their

cool mud pool. The smallest piglet
nuzzled around Kirsty and Rachel's
legs before he went. 'Thank you,'
he squealed happily.

Rachel watched them go. 'What
will happen to the goblin?' she
asked. 'He won't have to stay there
for ever, will he?'

Goldie's eyes twinkled
mischievously. 'Not for ever, no,' she
said. 'He'll get out of the mud
as soon as it rains.'
She smiled
cheerfully.

'Jack Frost won't be pleased with him when he finds out we've got the Sunshine Feather back, though!'

Now that they were out of danger, Goldie waved the Sunshine Feather with an expert flourish and the sun began to set – just as it was supposed to. The girls watched as the sky was flooded with orange and pink and a rich deep red.

'Let's take the Sunshine Feather back to Doodle,' Kirsty said happily.

'And then we'd better go to bed!'

Rachel was yawning. 'It's been another busy day, hasn't it?' she smiled.

With the sun setting, the warmth was quickly ebbing away and the girls soon found themselves shivering in their thin T-shirts. Goldie fluttered above them with the Sunshine Feather, tapping it gently to sprinkle a few sunbeams onto their bare arms to keep them warm.

It was almost dark by the time they got back to Kirsty's garden. They could just about see the silhouette of Doodle perched on the barn roof.

Goldie flew up to give the cockerel back his magic feather. As she did so, Doodle came to life, his fiery feathers glowing brilliant colours in the twilight. He turned to look at Rachel and Kirsty. 'Will come—' he squawked urgently. But, before he could say any more, the magic drained away, his colours faded and he became a rusty old weather-vane once again.

Each time the girls managed to

return one of Doodle's feathers, the cockerel came to life for a few brief moments and squawked a couple of words. Rachel frowned as she pieced together all the words that Doodle had said to them so far. 'Beware! Jack Frost will come...' she murmured, feeling an icy shiver down her spine as if Jack Frost was already there. 'It's a warning, Kirsty. Let's hope he's not coming soon!'

Goldie looked worried. 'Take care, girls. And thank you for everything,' she said. She blew them a stream of fairy kisses that sparkled in the darkening sky. 'I must go back to Fairyland now. Goodbye!'

Kirsty and Rachel watched Goldie fly away until she was nothing more than a tiny golden speck in the distance. Then, just as they were about to get ready for bed, they

heard footsteps and Mr Tate came out of the house. He was looking around, a puzzled expression on his face. 'Did I just hear a cockerel crowing?' he asked.

'A cockerel? At this time of day?' Kirsty replied innocently.

Mr Tate frowned. 'I must be hearing things,' he said, turning to go back inside. 'Good night, girls. Sleep well.' Then he glanced up at Doodle as he headed back towards the house. 'I'm sure that weather-vane had a smaller tail,' he muttered, then shook his head. 'Seeing things as well! Definitely time to call it a night...'

Kirsty and Rachel smiled at each other. 'Only three more feathers to find,' Kirsty said. 'I wonder which one will be next!'